Publisher: PIAOTT Publishing LLC, Chicago, IL

Sunbeams Through Poetry

Shirley Rice

Printed in the United States of America

©2022 by Library of Congress Cataloging-in-Publication Data

ISBN: 978-1-7362522-9-1

I0525158

PIAOTT
PUBLISHING & GRAPHIC DESIGN LLC.
PUT IT ALL ON THE TABLE BOOKS

SUNBEAMS THROUGH POETRY

Poetry, Creative Writing & Isms
By Minister Shirley Rice

To my beloved sister in the Gospel and cherished friend,
Elder Shirley A. Rice:

"And the Lord answered me, and said, "Write the vision, and make it plain upon tables, that he may run that readeth it. For the vision is yet for an appointed time, but at the end it shall speak, and not lie: though it tarry, wait for it; because it will surely come, it will not tarry." Habakkuk 2:2-3

A request to write a foreword to a novel or series of books is a daunting yet humbling task. It requires the writer to have some knowledge of the author's body of work, professional accomplishments, and personal interests. This responsibility also should involve some connection with the author whereby those who know them present a greater insight into who the author is and an honest analysis of their intent and purpose. More importantly, however, it motivates them to write and publish their works for many to read and gain something from it. Evangelist Shirley Rice is a Licensed and Ordained Minister, mother, wife, grandmother, vocalist, and author. Her latest book, Sunbeams through Poetry, is a compilation of inspirational quotes, original poems, and isms that contain prophetic words, wisdom, love, insight, and rays of sunlight from the heart and spirit of Elder Rice. Always guided by and obedient to the Spirit of God, Elder Shirley (affectionately called) sees and learns of the visions God has placed in her, plans, and executes those dreams and visions into words or songs that heal, deliver, and set free those who are bound by anything. I believe that Evangelist Shirley Rice, with her latest book, mirrors Scripture in that she has taken all inspiration and wisdom from what God has shown her and gone on to "write God's vision" and "made it plain, understandable," at an appointed time such as this, and it is so right on time! We are hurting in today's world and seem to be lacking in sympathy, love, and Christian values. Some are lost and discounted; some are disconnected or estranged from family, friends, and loved ones. I believe that these collections of poetry and other writings are what the world needs to read right now and be filled with the peace and love of God through Elder Shirley Rice's anointing in Sunbeams through Poetry. It will inspire, encourage, uplift any reader, and shine in their hearts and minds.

Reverend Adrienne D. Watson

PREFACE

*T*his book is composed of poems, quips, and quotes from KJV. Much of this material came to me in the night while my husband slept in bed. Before I go any further, I must acknowledge my dear friend in the Gospel, who did not hesitate when I called and asked her to write my foreword. Minister Adrienne Watson has been here for me. She became my sister in Christ when our churches began fellowshipping together. She had no idea that I was an ordained minister at the time. But that is another story to write.

I have always had a deep love of literature, Shakespeare, prose, and poetry. I recall as a freshman at J.W. Million H.S in the small town of Earlington, KY. One of my teachers, Mrs. N. McCain, had selected several of her students to write a thousand-word essay entitled "A Voice of Democracy." I had no idea where this essay was headed. However, after making many mistakes, I rephrased the sentence structure. I was very pleased with my final draft.

The final three students were chosen to represent our school on our local radio station. We practiced reading our essays, myself and two other students, until we were ready to speak over the radio airwaves. Frightening yes, sweaty palms yes! At least I can speak for myself. I placed third in the contest. Even though I did not finish first place, I was happy to compete and finish at the top. From that day forward, I enjoyed writing. Even things that sometimes do not make sense, no rhythm or rhyme usually come together. I have written many unpublished works that consist of plays, songs, sermons, and other material. I Thank God for the gifts that he has given me. I do not take it for granted. I went on to study speech and creative writing in college, which has helped perpetuate my writing skills. This book was written with you, the reader, in mind. Travel with me as the words come to life.

TABLE OF CONTENTS

GOOD MORNING GOD

Thank You for this amazing day! I Thank You for a peaceful night of rest.

Thank You for accompanying Your Holy angels around me, I do not know what this day will hold for me, but I know the holder and keeper of life.

Thank You for putting me on the path that will help me show others the love You have placed upon me.

Thank You for the insight to help others along the way. The people that we meet. These people might be co-workers, family, friends, strangers, professionals, or neighbors. They could be homeless, lonely, confused, or depressed.

We will come across many of these people. The bottom line is how we paint their character. NOW HOW SHOULD WE RESPOND?

People respond to acts of kindness. Did you know that many wealthy people have mutual gains and would gladly trade it for true love and affection?

Love, peace, joy, and patience cannot be bought.
We pursue happiness, but it will not last.

The thing that Christ gives us is free and will last all eternity.
God never put a price tag on the love He has given us.
He offers salvation.

Once you accept Him as Lord and Savior and begin to walk in His word, you are a new creature.

Whenever you feel like the things of this life are becoming overwhelming, call on Jesus. He is right there waiting to catch you before you fall.

God is ever present.
Nothing catches Him off guard.
He sees and knows it all.

Father God, Thank You for being constant in my life.

I Thank You for being the orchestrator of my life.
I Thank You each day You awaken me to fulfill all You have
commissioned me to do. Thank You for filling me with Your precious Holy
Ghost.

I realize that without You, I am lost. Without You, my life is not worth
living.

Yes, I realize that the things we are witnessing are undesirable to some.
Many today have never witnessed what was happening in the land before
the coronavirus started.

The destroying and dismantling of families, killing of African American
people, and protests of every kind and source.

Police brutality and hostility against law and order, unemployment rates
are sparing, children being murdered on the streets and in drive-bys,
parents being shot while children are in the back seat of their car, mayors
of cities and governors of state are at their wit's end, the economy is down,
looters and robbers are destroying businesses and livelihood, churches
closed, members unable to attend services, virtual media services are
taking the place of traditional in house service, people are afraid to leave
their homes.

People are crying out, but who's listening? How long, Oh Lord, must we
sit and be silent?

What A Mighty God!

You're not just ordinary. You are extraordinary. When God made you, you were made in His image. You were made to rule over everything that He created, and He said that was very good. Genesis 1:31 NIV "God saw all that He had made, and it was very good. And there was evening, and there was morning, the sixth day."

God gave us everything that we need to survive in His world.

Why are we destroying what we did not have the ability to create?

The love that God saw when He created the universe, the sky, the sun, moon, and stars.

The light He called day and the dark He called night.

He put everything in its own space, and everything that is alike, He put in its space.

He called the water to come forth and fill the space where water could flow and the dry land, He kept dry and solid.

He made every kind of seed for its kind to be able to continue to reproduce, every plant He made that we can eat.

He provided animals for food and clothing and trees for shelter.

Birds, every creepy thing, nothing was left undone.

You never have to worry about who God is.

Open your bible and read the first chapter of Genesis.

Creation and the beginning of time.

The World Is All A STAGE

The world is all a stage, each individual acting out a scene.

Have you decided what character you will be today?

Will it be something or someone you can live with for the rest of your life?

The scene you play will either help lift you into the atmosphere or it can hinder you from moving forward.

Think before you act.

The choice is yours!

DARE I LOOK BACK

Dare I look back on yesterday,
With all of its broken promises.

Its practicalities, heartaches
and pain!

Dare I think of what could
have been or what would
have been and all of its
missed opportunities.

Dare I allow myself to hope
for tomorrow and look back
on shattered dreams!

Life is filled with many
misses and mistakes of what
could have been and what
should have been!

But when you fill it with
God's rich abundance, His
righteousness, and His
promises, your outlook
becomes brightened, and your
load becomes lighter.

Broken promises welcome
realities, heartache, and pain far
and in between. And what would
have been, and what should have
been have since diminished.

Dare I look back!

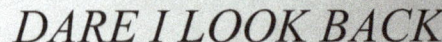

12

AWAKE

Awake, awake!

From your sleep.

All you who are weary.

All you that are despondent.

Awake, for the long dreary days have passed.

Behold, the sun is shining.

A new day is dawning.

Awake from your slumbers, awake!

WHO AM I?

Who am I? I cannot tell.

I know that I have a story to tell.

One that was created and given to me by our Heavenly Father.

It is my duty to tell others about who HE is.

Allowing His light to shine in me that others will see,

His good awakens through me.

Thank JESUS

I ponder in my spirit.

Where I would be, had not Jesus died and had not
He been resurrected from the grave, I would be
lost like a ship without a sail.

My life would go nowhere.

I would be subjected to the law, where judges
and rules dictate.

When the veil was ripped, it no longer separated
us from God, we no longer had to go before man,
but we could go directly to the Lord.

GOOD EASTER MORNING

I stand here on this Blessed Resurrection Sunday to encourage your hearts.

I want you to know that no matter what situation you're going through, that it does not matter how bleak the outcome looks to you.

I know a man who died for your sins and for my sins, and He rose on the third day, with all power, holding that power in His hands.

Take heart, my brother and sister, just know that Jesus lives.

We have everything that we need.

REJOICE

Rejoice that God is not short of His word.

If you need healing and the doctor has given up on you.

I know a man from Galilee who can heal you from all manner of sickness and disease.

If you need a financial blessing, help with that wayward child, or it could be that you are in mourning today or the bank is about to foreclose and your mortgage is due, and you feel your back is against the wall.

Just look to Jesus where all your help comes from; turn it over, and HE will work it out.

WHAT WILL IT TAKE?

Women, what will it take for us to wake up before it's too late,

We sometimes are our own worst enemies.

We are self-absorbed.

We talk about each other and seldom hand out a compliment to one another.

We gossip and murmur about one another. "Look at her! She thinks she's all that. Ain't about nothing."

When are we going to lift up each other?

It's not about fame or fortune. It's not about your long, straight, or wavy hair, it's not about your manicured fingernails, it's not about your stilettos, it's not about your designer handbag and shoes, it's not about that fancy car that you drive.

It's not about your fat bank account. It's not about your degrees or what top ten schools you attended.

It's not about that house that sits high on a hill or low in the valley.

It's not about you being in charge of a handful of people; you don't even own the company.

It's not about the man that rocks your world,

But; it's all about Jesus, the one who sacrificed and gave His life for us. That through Him, we might be saved and have eternal life.

WHEN GOD IS IN THE BUILDING

When God is in the building, every heart will rejoice.
When God is in the building, there will be one voice.
When God is in the building, every hand lifts in praise.
When God is in the building, every sin will be erased.
When God is in the building, no more sorrow or pain.
When God is in the building, every life will be changed.
When God is in the building, every soul is rearranged.
When God is in the building, every heart is the same.

Put your trust in Jesus; let Him have His way.
Put your trust in the Master each and every day.

GET INVOLVED

Where were you when the votes were cast?

Did you sit back and say, "No need to vote, nothing will change"?

Were you one of those who refused to register to vote?

Were you a spectator, watching to see what would take place?

Whatever your reason, just know your vote counts.

IF your candidate was not elected, look at yourself and not
at others.

Many protestors who were upset about the outcome did not vote.

If you want change, let your voice be heard before the event.

We must learn to live and work in perfect peace.
Jesus is our leader and guide.

Look what the haters did to Him, yet He committed no sin.

He went about teaching and preaching, healing, feeding, and
forgiving others.

Telling all about His father, proving to others that there is no
greater love than a man who would lay down His life for a friend
and to love our neighbor as we love ourselves.

THE SPLENDOR OF A TREE

Her back is bent as her limbs sway from
side to side, trying to withstand the
fierce winds and the heavy-laden
snow upon her branches.

She has stood for many years.
As a brave soldier going off to
work.

To protect her environment, her
defense shields her from the gusty
winds and aids us by providing shelter.

When all is serene, she allows us to
sleep upon her wooden trunk and sit
upon her wooden throne.

LOVE IS

Love is God knitting us into the beautiful place of our mother's womb.

Love is a masterpiece of God.

Love is earth, a collection of beautiful colors splitting through the spectrum of light rays.

Love is unchanging; it finds beauty in all that is created. It is not prideful or boastful.

Love is pure; it is not devilish. It gives all that it has.

Love is laughter in a child.

Love is watching someone grow old gracefully.

Love is sharing a kiss, embracing in a hug.

Love is finding joy in oneself.

Love is never having to hear someone say, "I'm sorry."

Love is innocent.

Love is giving the shoes off your feet while you are also someone without.

Love is finding beauty in others.

Love is helping a friend who no longer has the energy to take care of the things they love to do.

Love is opening the door to let someone in.

Love is calling a friend daily.

Love is enduring.

Love is God, the very essence of our being.

Love is me giving back a part of what God has blessed me with.

Love is taking time out of your busy schedule to help others.

Love is praying for better and then receiving unexpected blessings.

Love is comforting others when they have lost a loved one.

Love is peace.

Love is helping others when they do not have enough money to make a purchase.

Love is helping a stranded motorist along the roadside.

Love is helping a stray dog or cat when its owner has abandoned it.

Love is God helping me up when I was unable to hold myself.

LEARN TO BE A FIGHTER

Encouraging words lift and inspire us to go
forward when we are at our lowest.

We need to read, see, hear, and know everything
will be alright.

Sometimes life will throw us a curve ball, and
we cannot catch it, or our faith is not strong
enough to sustain us.

It's good when you have friends there to hold us
when we cannot find our way.

I Thank God for you, dear friends.

THE GREATEST LOVE

The Greatest love is the love that Jesus gave us all at Mount Calvary where He hung, bled, and died for our sins.

A man that came to know us along the way.
A man that hung between two thieves, and one of them cried out, "Oh Lord, remember me when You come into Your kingdom.

Love is Jesus telling the man, you will be with me in paradise.

What love.
What humility.

Love is building up and never tearing down. Love is a new adventure. Love is getting to know a new friend. Love is sin at its worst and God at His best.

God gave His very best for us.
He gave His only begotten son.

What is love; it's Jesus at the cross for our redemption from sin.
A long-lasting love that is open for all, valiant, everlasting, pure, and innocent.

When someone asks you, what love is, just say Jesus.
Which is unconditional love.

ACCEPT ME

Please do not go changing.

Accept me for who I am.

Find the beauty that lies within.

Please do not go changing or
rearranging me; get to know me.

Don't judge me or put me down.

I've had enough of that to last a
lifetime, enough criticism to go
around the wall.

Accept me for who I really am.

I AM A WINNER

Look deep inside of yourself.

No matter where you are in life.
No matter what you are faced with in life.
No matter what others put upon you.

Tell yourself, "I'm a winner, you
can't stop me, and you can't hold me
down."

Step out of your comfort zone.
Step out of your fear.

Tell yourself, "I am a winner!"

THIS IS ME SAYING GOODBYE

Goodbye to all the hurt and pain of life.

Goodbye to the one who told me I was the one, the love of His life.

Goodbye to the man who said we will always be,

Goodbye to the lies and the liars.

Goodbye to the fears.

Goodbye to the neighbor who moved away and promised to keep in touch.

Goodbye to the so-called friend.

Goodbye to all the drama.

Goodbye to the failed relationships.

Goodbye to foolishness.

Goodbye to all the bullies in life.

This is me saying goodbye to all the negativities.

Goodbye to anger.

Goodbye to the dream changers and the dream crushers.

This is me saying hello to the new and reinvented me.

SENDING DAILY REMINDERS

"Thank You, Dear Lord, for sending me daily reminders of Your love.

Your love and care for me is often shown through a friend or a loved one.

Recently, I was in severe pain.

Although I had been prescribed medication by my pain physician, the medicine did not stop me from being in pain.

A dear friend sent me healing prayers and Scripture.

I began to feel so much better.

Nothing can heal us like the words of God.

Because of You, dear God, we are constantly reminded of how deep Your love for us truly is.

NO MORE PROCRASTINATION

Don't put off today for tomorrow. Get all you can out of today, for tomorrow is not promised. It may never come. We say, "I have tomorrow. Tomorrow I'll do this or that." When in reality, we don't know if we will see tomorrow. We may not see tomorrow. Only Jesus knows who holds our tomorrow. It is He who made us. Many opportunities have died simply because we procrastinate today for tomorrow. Learn to live life to its fullest and be the best you can be today.

BEING AN OVERCOMER

Press on even when your mind tells you to give up.

Hold on even when things appear to be impossible.

The hardship is not given to the strong (swift); the hardship is given to the one who can endure (hold on) to the end.

Stop telling yourself, I can't.

Start telling yourself I can.

I can make it even when things look dim, and there seems to be no way out. I simply look to the hill from where my help lies.

I am an overcomer.

LOVE AT THE CROSS

There is much love at the cross.

Jesus gave all that He had for us at the Calvary cross.

When I reflect on this time of treason, it brings
tears to my eyes.

What agony, sorrow, and shame.

A man who gave everything for us had
to go through, and yet through it all, He
endured all the ridicule, hatred, suffering,
and pain just to save us from our sins
and all that He asked us to do is
to "love one another" and
to learn to love our
neighbor as
one.

A MOTHER'S LOVE

A mother's love is pure and deep.

She thinks of you while you're asleep.

From a baby in her arms and then on her knee.

When you have your family,

you will reflect on the days that
used to be

that beautiful treasure that came
from no other

than your dear mother.

A FATHER'S LOVE

Some call them fathers.

Some call them dad or daddy.

Some even call them pop or pops.

Some even refer to their dad as poppie.

Whatever name you call the man that you've come to know as "dad", he is the one who will help guide you through life's ups and downs and turnarounds.

It takes a special man to own up to his responsibilities, to help the babe grow into a man, to tell his daughter, I want the very best for you.

He is a responsible leader and ensures his family has everything they need.

It is the man who teaches his son how to navigate through life.

He teaches his son how to become a real man; he is affectionate to his wife.

He teaches his daughter to shine, love, and dream big dreams.

He tells his children that all things are possible when you believe.

He tells his child each person is different and not to settle for less.

Be the best you can be.

Be successful; always pursue higher education and higher career goals.

Work, don't expect others to do for you what you can do for yourself.

He teaches them to buy only what they can afford; pay as they go.

He teaches you to save money as a child; you learn responsibilities growing up at home.

He teaches the skills and knowledge that will carry you through life.

Whoever your dad is, however, he came to be your dad; love him. Appreciate the man you call dad.

A dad is not only the one who is your biological birth parent. But he is the one who is, and always someday, you can depend upon.

No matter when you need him, he's there.

He is there to say, "I love you. I'm here for you."

He spends valuable time with you and your family.

He's there when you learn to drive, go to the prom, graduate, and pursue higher expectations.

A dad will never leave you; you can always depend on him when you need him.

SHOWING ON MY FACE

I once saw the old become older, and the young
seemingly were carefree.

But as time passed, I could see myself gradually
changing through the years.

All of life's frustration, bitterness, hurt, and pain
began to show through my face.

Weary of what could have been, or should have,
that never took place.

Seeing life through the dreams of others but not
pursuing the dreams of self-fulfillment.

Life is like a jungle sometimes.

You can't see your way through.

COVER US

Cover us, Dear Lord, as we go throughout this day.

Lead, guide, and protect in a very special way.

When we awake, let us feel Your joy.

When we are sad, help us feel Your presence.

Speak to our hearts, Dear Lord.

When life comes to us in unexpected and unusual ways.

Help us to know that You are there standing upright.

When our world has suddenly collapsed around us, give us strength, Dear Lord, to endure all that is placed upon us.

We need Your touch.

We need Your love.

Teach us to give love and to receive love.

Cover us as we go throughout each day.

Show us Your perfect way.

IF I COULD

If I could, I'd shield you from the storms in your life.

If I could, I would solve all of your problems.

If I could, I would put a smile upon your face.

If I could, I would tell you to watch out for the strange that lurks about,

If I could, I would watch your every step; teach you the fundamentals of life.

If I could, I would pick up the phone to say hello.

If I could, I'd wipe the tears from your face.

If I could, I'd tell you about a better place.

If I could, I would shower you with hugs and kisses.

If I could, you would feel love each and every day.

If I could, I would tell you all about life.

Since I cannot warn you about that danger that lurks about and all around.

I'll love you while I can; I will tell you every day how much you mean to me and what a difference you are making in this life.

So whatever path you take, know this, Jesus will be your guide when you're lost.

He is your life, your joy, you're all. Know that when all others forsake you, Jesus will hold you up.

God is always there when parents and others cannot be.

So my child, when you don't know what to do, and your friends are few, just say Jesus.

Whenever you lose your way and don't know what to say.

Call on the name of Jesus. He'll be there; whenever you need Him. "Life is like a mist, and then it's no more."

STOP THE VIOLENCE

One heart, one beat; thrump de thrump.

STOP THE VIOLENCE

So much anger, so much pain

We need sunshine and rain.

One heart, one beat; thrump de thrump.

Teardrops falling like rain, too much gun violence,
so much pain.

We need sunshine and rain.

One heart, one beat; thrump de thrump.

We need joy and peace.

STOP THE VIOLENCE.

WE KOOL LIKE THAT

We kool like that, that's what the young folks say.

They'll be together till their dying day.

We Kool like that until you're faced with certain uncertainties,

We Kool like that, but you won't take me home to meet your mama.

Our paths are different when we cross the street.

You live on White Street, and I live on Black Avenue, on the opposite sides.

You say it's better on your side of the street, but when I finally crossed over to your side of the street, your side didn't seem better than mine.

I found greed, jealousy, lying, manipulation, and power in the wrong hands, people stepping over each other to get what they wanted.

My side of the street was content with people laughing, children playing, and neighbors sharing what they had with one another.

People spoke to one another as they approached or passed along their way.

People are satisfied knowing Jesus and having Him in their life.

Just knowing that Jesus could deliver them out of every situation, just hearing Jesus wasn't enough, but having a real relationship with Him would outlast everything that this life could give.

We Kool like that.

GOD IS GREATER
THAN OUR CIRCUMSTANCES

Our circumstances are no match for our God.

As believers of Christ, we realize that our problems are minimal because we are deeply rooted in our faith and believe every word of God.

Our faith will pull us through all difficulties in life.

We are strong when problems arise.

We say, "Greater is He that is within me than who is within the world."

We realize that weeping will only endure for just a little while and that God will wipe every tear from our eyes.

Trust in Jesus when you cannot see your way.

Learn to call out to Him.

He will hear your every call.

Seek Him while you can.

He is waiting to hear from you.

A NEW BEGINNING

A very good friend informs my husband and me that they are moving.
I was very disheartened when I heard the news.

Good and faithful members in the church, both he and his wife.

Very loyal and trustworthy friends, in good standings with the church.

Both are youth Sunday school teachers, active in bible study and
vacation bible school.

Both can sing.

I stopped and thought about all the good they have done to help the
church and the community.

God is rewarding them for their labor.

Even though it is difficult to see them leave, I know that God is
thrusting them forward into the next chapter of their lives.

Even greater things they will do. Be blessed, my friends.

STAY TRUE TO YOURSELF

Don't give anybody else your power, be who you are and believe in yourself. Life dreams can come true. Never allow anyone to determine your path. Prove to others that you are better than what they say about you. Find your purpose in life. It's a great life if you stay true to yourself and God.

EVERYTHING I NEED
IS IN JESUS CHRIST

In
the world
that we live in,
we find ourselves being
jealous of things that we did
not bring about or create.

The problems we are often confronted with are
generated by others who do not have people's best
interests in view.

So many suffer at the hands of people whose interests and
concerns are badly about themselves.

So many families have been torn apart by the careless act
of violence and instinctual blindness inflicted upon families
everywhere.

Knowing that all we need can be found in Jesus Christ is
wonderful.

No matter what the problem, the resolve is in Him.

Lord, LET YOUR LIGHT SHINE IN ME

As I awake on this day, allow Your light to shine in me; as I greet others throughout today, allow Your presence to live in me.

I need You to bless me, Lord.
I need a tender touch from You, Lord.

Somebody, somewhere, needs to feel Your presence.

The world's a stage; we are the lights to help build others up when they're down.

Allow them to see Your light in us.

Help us, as Your children, to bring light to a dark place, where light is not fluttering through.

Lord, let Your light shine in me!

A FAITHFUL PRAYER

Dear Lord, You know our ends and outs and our turnabouts.

You know our thoughts from afar.

In You, we trust, we flourish.

Help us in our daily walk to be faithful and truthful in what we do for You!

We are Your ambassadors; help us to tell everyone that we know about You.

A man who can save our souls.

A man who can keep us from seen and unseen dangers.

Thank you for all You do for us.

PROMISE

We Thank You, Dear Lord, for Your promise towards us.

We Thank You that we can come to You in prayer.

We Thank You that when we are broken, torn apart, leaving destruction behind and all around, you bring restoration.

Our hope and faith are renewed through You and in You.

We Thank You for being omnipotent, the great You are; our redeemer, our way maker, our peace, our love and joy of this life.

We Thank You for being our Master, our Lord, and our Savior, ruler overall.

Thank You for being infallible; never changing, always the same.

We Thank You, Dear Lord, for security.

Shielding us.

Protecting us.

Watching over us.

Keeping us safe from all hurt, harm, and danger.

We Thank You, dear Lord, that you are eternal.

You are the same today and forever.

You are Alpha, our beginning.

You are Omega, our ending, the first, and the last.

You are our PROMISE!

CREATION

The best creation was made by none other than God!

God created this earth, the world, and all that is within. He made the sun and the moon and caused the sun to give us daylight and the moon to glow at night, shining throughout the night.

He created the mountains where men step to conquer by climbing to the peak. The great tablet where presidents have been carved into the stones. Where people come to stop and look at the view.

But He didn't stop there.

The hills, valleys, water streaming from the hilltops, the deep blue sea, rivers, the stars in the sky that twinkles brightly at night, the trees, lilies in the field, and every flower God made.

The ins and outs of nature, He created every fruit tree, every notable plant, every type of grain, and every animal God created.

It is God who created man and mankind (woman).

There is absolutely nothing in this world that God did not have a hand in creating. The gold, silver, copper, all of the diamond mines, and gemstones are all His.

This world and all there is belongs to God.

What man can cause the sun to shine or the moon and stars to come out at night or bring down rain to cleanse the earth and have enough for our entire universe.

Nobody but the Lord who can guarantee food for the entire land?

Nobody but the Lord.

Who created every kind of tree or plant root for medical purposes?

Nobody but God.

Who created every kind of animal and mammal?

Nobody but God.

PRAYER OF PRAISE

Most Holy, Almighty God, Thank You for another day. Thank You for taking charge over us and for sending Your Holy angels. Thank You for protecting us as we slumbered and slept through the night. That's another reason to praise Your Holy name. That's enough to say "Thank You"; Thank You, dear Lord, for blessing us with a sound mind, eyes to see, ears to hear, legs to walk, and a mouth to talk. We Say Thank You.

BLESSINGS OF TODAY

Today I lift my hands and give my all to the Lord.

Today I will live without grumbling or complaints.

Today I will love all that I meet, great each one in Godly love,

Today I will help to cheer up my brothers and sisters.

Today I will send lots of good wishes to those who have lost their way.

Send a cheery note; sing a song of God's amazing grace.

Today I will tell a child that they can grow up to be whatever they desire to be when they put Christ first.

Today I will pray for those who say mean things about me and others, ask the Lord to forgive them, and ask God to help me not harbor resentment towards them.

Today I will read the word of God; Sing songs of joy.

Today I will lift and inspire others.

Today, I will be the very best that I can be.

In Jesus' name, Amen.

RISE ALONE

Sometimes the accusations that are hurled your way can bring you down.

We must never forget that our Savior did nothing to warrant this maliciousness sent His way.

Yet, a man of no sin; endured all unrighteousness, even death, to save us from our sins.

Even on the cross, He asked His Father to forgive them for they know not know what they do.

So, when we find ourselves in similar situations, ask yourself, "What would Jesus do?"

So never give in to conclusions, allowing our thoughts to outweigh the good that lies deep inside us.

EMPOWER ME

Empower me, Lord, to do Your work today.
I ask You to strengthen me along my way.
Help me to be the best that I can be.

Please, Lord, take me by my hand and help me to
not allow life to hinder me but to march forward in
victory.

Teach me, Dear Lord, not to complain but to always
proclaim Your Holy name.

KNOW YOURSELF

Negative people can and will often take up all the air surrounding you. Don't allow people to drain your positive outlook. Ask yourself who you are surrounding yourself with. Do you have friends who will lift you or trust in you? Are they the ones who never have anything good to say about others? Watch out for the company that you're keeping so they won't falter their negative influences on you.

JESUS IS STRONGER

We have witnessed and gone through so much as we reflect on our lives. Some move on, and others stay stagnant. However, we have kept God's grace and tender mercy. Along this journey, there has been joy, sorrow, sadness, pain, and great loss; Loss of family, spouse, parent, loss of a child, while others have lost jobs, homes, relationships, finances, and friends. No matter what you have gone through, the great thing is that you are an overcomer; you're never alone in pain. Jesus is stronger and greater than all our circumstances.

Sometimes in life, losses can allow blessings. God has always had better for us. While we hold on, we cannot let go of many things, but our God rids us of negativity and gives us new beginnings.

Where there is loss, there is hope.

Where there is sorrow, there is joy.

When hatred arrives, peace thrives.

Where there is pain, there is God's strength.

Take a walk with Jesus. Stop holding onto the old and familiar. Walk in 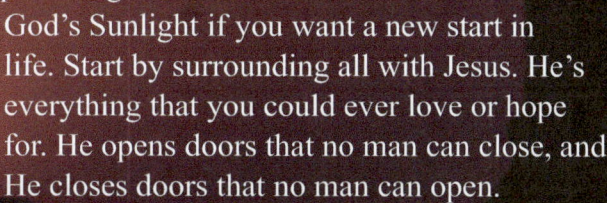 God's Sunlight if you want a new start in life. Start by surrounding all with Jesus. He's everything that you could ever love or hope for. He opens doors that no man can close, and He closes doors that no man can open.

Your life will never be the same.

A BUMPY FLIGHT

Truly God is great and is to be praised.

We have been blessed by the best.

There's nobody like our God!

Nobody can compare or even come close to Him!

This has been a very bumpy flight, but God guided us; He held us and kept us from all hurt, harm, and danger.

We may have been bruised along the way, hurt, not broken.

Thank Jesus.

We fall down, but You, Lord,
picked us up.

You didn't leave us in our distress; You
stood with us all to fly high again. Thank You, my
King.

You stood tall when my back was against the wall and never let me fall.

Thank You, Jesus, for helping us find ourselves again.

You loved us unconditionally, and this I say Thank You!

Much love.

Let us look forward with new hope, dreams, and admiration in Jesus' name, knowing there is no problem that God cannot resolve.

BE STILL AND LISTEN

Sometimes in life, you must be still and learn to listen to that quiet voice.

When people say mean things to you for no reason, don't try to get even with them or go word for word.

Still away from your secret place in the cloud, learn to obey God.

Meditate on Him, learn His Word, and pray as often as the spirit leads you.

God has a journey for you to travel; you must be willing to follow Him.

He has plans for you to reach mountains to climb, new people to meet, and new opportunities to explore.

He's telling you that the ocean has no ending, and the sea has no depth.

It is never ending.

Just as the ocean and the sea are never ending, so is His word.

God's word will never pass away.

Don't give up; keep on believing in God.

GOD'S GIFT IS THE GIFT OF LIFE

Do you realize that each day we awake is a gift of God?

Each day we are blessed by the power of God.

We are all blessed in various ways.

God blesses us according to our individual needs.

There is nobody that can provide for us the way that God does!

Without Him, we could not raise our arms: there would be no activity of our mind, body, or soul.

No emotions, no movements without God.

Serving God is one of the best things we can do for Him.

Loving His children and caring for them, blessing others as Jesus puts His blessing upon us.

Don't you know that there is nothing too hard for God?

God's Gift lasts forever when you are obedient to Him.

THE GIFT THAT KEEPS GIVING

Every day we awake is another gift the Lord has blessed us with.

Jesus is the light of the world.

His light is love; His Gift is the eternal Salvation.

We are truly blessed each day to be given another gift.

We receive a new gift each day; how we choose to use this Gift is solely left to us.

We can use it to spread happiness, joy, and peace, or we can use it to spread violence, evil, or destruction.

God gave this Gift to you to be a light in the darkness.

Don't waste what He has freely given you today.

Walk in LOVE.

GIVE GOD HIS CHURCH BACK

We who have been called by His name should worship God in true holiness, not be swayed by the things of this world, for we who believed in Him know that whatsoever we need, You will provide. You own it all. Help us to keep our eyes on You, Lord Jesus.

Not giving in to every whim and doctrine that comes along.

For you, our Father has given us all that we need.

It's not about us; it's all about You.

Help us to stay focused on You and You alone.

We have made God's House too commercial.

WHERE IS THE PRAISE?

When will we make Jesus the center of our praise so those walking in darkness can begin to see the true light of God?

The question is, when are we, who are called by His name, going to give God His church back?

We don't need symbolism or gimmicks.

We need the preached word of God and the presence of the Lord.

We've tried the world's way of doing things, and we, as believers, know it didn't work.

WHAT HAPPENED TO SAINTS?

When we praised and worshipped God?

When we were excited for Sunday to come?

What took your joy and your trust in God away?

We came ready to serve the Lord.

We greeted each one with a Holy kiss and hug.

When did you stop loving Him the way that He loves you?

It is time that God's House became what He designated it to be; a House Of Praise!

His House should always represent His power, might, love, joy, peace, and kindness towards us.

Prayer and His Holy Word are the priority.

When we give God's House back to Him, broken hearts will be made whole again.

When God's House is returned to Him, sickness will be alleviated.

When God's House is restored back to Him, deliverance will take place, restoration is restored, forgiveness takes place, belief is restored, worries are erased, and stony hearts are given brand new life.

Come into His House with praise and worship.

God deserves all the glory, honor, and praise, for it is His and His alone.

Lord'S FIELD

Master, can I work in Your field today?

As I work in Your field today, I see lots of remnants that have been left behind. I see broken hearts to be mended and lost souls to save.

As I glean along the way, I walk a little further, and a mother is kneeling, praying over her son, who just walked away, and not even a goodbye was said.

I see a father pleading with his son to go home, telling him you have a home and people who love you; you don't have to be out there by yourself.

I walk a little further, there is a preacher who turned from his church, and another left his wife and family for another woman.

I go a little further, and there is a child who has been abused by her mother and father. She is crying out, why did you misuse me? Why did you beat me and tell me to live in a cage?

Yet as I continued to gleam, I saw children and young adults who had been sold into child labor and prostitution.

As I go further, there is a mother and father who can't pay their bills or buy food for their family.

Toward the end of the field, a family is looking for a better way of life, immigrants are being turned around, and children are separated from their parents, living in undesirable circumstances.

At the end of our labor, I hear our father guiding us to come to Him, all that are weary and lost in spirit, I will turn your hardships into something beautiful, I love you, I care about you, Turn to me I'll make everything alright.

JUST NOW

I wrote this poem when I was going through a rough time in my life.

I had just parted with a man I had known all my life.

A man who was strong and courageous.

A man that sacrificed all he could for his wife and children.

A man who walked me to school on my first day and brought my favorite lunch every day.

A man who stood by me through thick and thin.

One Sunday, I had returned home from church, sitting at my kitchen table, these words came to me, and I began to write.

Just now, I give my life to You.

Just now, my life is made brand new.

Just now, dark clouds have faded away, and I owe it all to You.

Just now, no more loneliness awaits.

Just now, my days are bright and cheery, and I owe it all to You.

I Thank You, Lord, for blessing me with a father that truly loved my siblings and me.

A man with no former education stood with dignity, and grace made it possible.

We graduated from high school and continued to pursue higher education.

Thank You, Heavenly Father, for my dearly beloved dad, who will always live in my heart.

GOOD MORNING AND HAPPY DAY

Today is a good day!

You ask me how?

Because we serve the King of kings and the Lord of Lords.

He is good every day, brand new mercies He gives daily.

Jesus has everything that we need.

WHAT'S IN A NAME?

A name is meaningful, usually given by a father or mother before or after the birth of a child.

A name should be prayed about and given great thought before tagging it or attaching it to your child.

You must remember that the name you choose should not be a name that will cause your child to be bullied, ridiculed, or made to feel ashamed.

The name you choose should carry weight, volume, and character.

It should be a name that carries power and symbolizes wealth.

A strong name exuberant, full of energy, excitement, and cheerfulness.

Their faith will not allow circumstances to unravel and will stand strong in the midst of amity.

You will walk in the newness of life.

He will give new energy and an anointed life.

Do you lead God's people?

A strong name will inhibit God in all we do and say.

A strong name: male or female, will be a witness to Jesus and allow His Holy Spirit to lead the way, will be loyal, will listen closely to hear God through the message that is given by others, and will display God's character of home at school at work in the community and when ministering publicly to others.

God's light will shine bright; His light will be seen and shine bright in others. His Holy Spirit will be our leader and guide.

The name given to us will not be ashamed to tell others about God's power.

The name that God has blessed us to carry will bring youth and produce men and women who have been hidden from the world.

As we preach and teach about Jesus Christ, no other name is given to us that is all-powerful, all-knowing, and all-seeing like that of our Lord and Savior, Jesus Christ.

He is Alpha and Omega, The Beginning, and The End.

SUMMER

The summer was long and hot, and many families vacationed near and far away.

A dream of a lifetime, many worked double shifts and overtime to have the money to enjoy a carefree vacation, while others stayed at home and took getaways to nearby towns and neighboring cities.

Summer is a playful, carefree season with children enjoying the outdoors and parents wishing it would soon end.

Labor Day is the last summer holiday.

It's time to hit the road, fill the trunk, and reach your destination.

No matter the transportation, you can't wait to arrive at your favorite destinations.

Along our journey, we meet many people, some pleasant and engaging while others are not caring.

Summer is when we don't have to worry about many things; summer is laid back and relaxing.

We spend most of our time outdoors, perfecting our lawns and homes, working in our gardens, caring for our loved ones, and preparing for the cold winter months.

HOW AWESOME IS OUR GOD?

We work, and yet He allows us to rest.

I AM DAMAGED

Lord, I am damaged.

Make me whole again.

I am broken, feeling a disconnect from family and friends and sometimes from the one that created me.

Heal me, Dear Lord, mold, shape, and make me new again.

As believers, we know that many things we ask of the Lord have already been given to us. We must learn to reach deep inside our minds knowing that God will supply all of our needs.

Teach me to walk in the newness of life, teach me to redirect my thoughts, and not allow my judgment to become cloudy.

Bless me with good energy to do my daily tasks without the thought of how it will get done.

But know that You, God, are more than any of my circumstances.

Yes, I may ponder in my spirit and think I am damaged, but I know the one who is a restorer of life.

I know that He is the greatest.

I've seen Him work for the life of myself and others.

I know that with God, ALL THINGS ARE POSSIBLE.

AFTER THE PRAISE

After the praise brings joy, peace, healing, and deliverance.

Unexpected blessings spring forth like mighty water.

God inhabits the praise of His people.

PRAISE HIM.

When you praise Him in the storm of life, He will deliver you peace.

When you come out, give **Him The Glory** for what He did.

God Alone Is Worthy Of All The Honor And All The Glory.

After the praise, reflect on your mindset and walk boldly in it.

LEARNING TO FORGIVE

How can you forgive one another when others can make it difficult to forgive? Because the love of God lives deep inside of us.

A true disciple of God can look beyond the persecutor's fault and see them as they are.

What we see is not the person we know but the spirit operating inside them.

Help us, Dear Lord, to not judge one another's past failures, but love our brothers and sisters as Christ loves them.

We are fragile people who need the love that Jesus freely gives.

Bless and strengthen us when we become broken and need love.